PRAISE FOR
GOD'S LEFTOVERS

"*God's Leftovers* is not for the faint of heart. This brutal, visceral, shocking work of fiction is Ketchum meets Barker with a sprinkling of classic slashers and grindhouse pulp. If you want to be disgusted and unsettled, tapping into the vibe of films like *Martyrs*, *I Spit on Your Grave*, and *Texas Chainsaw Massacre*—this is your jam. I need to take a shower and douse myself in holy water."—Richard Thomas, author of *Spontaneous Human Combustion* and Bram Stoker Award® nominee

"If you can picture *The Hills Have Eyes* imbued with Jodorowsky's psychedelic sensibilities, you might get something close to *God's Leftovers*. With it, Grant Wamack makes a spectacular, bloody entrance into the splatterpunk arena. You've gotta read this book!" —Lucas Magnum, author of *Gods of the Dark Web*

"Deadly secrets, psychedelic drugs, sex magic... Wamack knows a thing or two about hard times and in this novella, you see life itself staring back at you, brandishing your worst fears, daring you to turn the page. I've been following Grant Wamack's work for a long time and *God's Leftovers* is his calling card, proving he's at the peak of his powers." — Michael J. Seidlinger, author of *Anybody Home?*

"Elements of the religious ecstatic, memorable characters, and a Dionysian climax with a perfect ending thrilled me. The sexual violence triggered and appalled me. The necrophilia, cannibalism, castration, rape, and someone wearing someone's else intestines like gold chains all absolutely disgusted me. Triggering, appalling, disgusting, thrilling— I am so happy Grant Wamack is writing again!" —Laura Lee Bahr, author of *Angel Meat*

GOD'S LEFTOVERS

GRANT WAMACK

ISBN: 978-1-68510-059-9 (sc)
ISBN: 978-1-68510-060-5 (ebook)

First printing edition: August 26, 2022
Printed by Bizarro Pulp Press in the United States of America.
Cover Design and Layout: Don Noble
Edited by Nick Day
Proofreading and Interior Layout by Scarlett R. Algee

Bizarro Pulp Press, an imprint of JournalStone Publishing
3205 Sassafras Trail
Carbondale, Illinois 62901

Bizarro Pulp Press books may be ordered through booksellers or by contacting:

JournalStone | www.journalstone.com

Dedicated to Brian McNaughton

GOD'S LEFTOVERS

PROLOGUE

Nicole Baranov ran through the desert with fire in her lungs and the bitter taste of sweat in her mouth. Her tongue felt like a dry weight and her teeth rattled with each step. She held her left side, ignoring the sweat dripping into her eyes as she fled across the dry wasteland, wondering if hell itself was on her heels.

She spat out a wad of mucus and wiped her cracked lips.

"FUCK THIS."

...

Four days, six hours and fifty-five minutes ago, she was navigating her 2012 Honda Odyssey through the outskirts of California on her way to Nevada. Her husband held up a water-stained brochure with the words VALLEY OF FIRE emboldened across the top in a cheesy yellow font. Nicole had stumbled across the endearing attraction while watching the Travel Channel. She immediately scribbled it down in her bucket-list book with a bright red pen. The following morning, she pitched the trip to her family and they were all onboard.

"So listen to this...among the species of wildlife you can see in the Valley of Fire are coyotes, ravens, bighorn sheep, badgers, white-tailed antelope, squirrels, rattlesnakes, ring-tailed cats and some desert tortoises. Isn't that cool?"

The children sitting in the back exclaimed in unison and her husband Tybee squeezed her shoulder. She smiled, feeling good about this decision. She had no idea why she got an uneasy feeling after initially booking the trip. Everything was flowing smoothly.

She parked the car and the whole family got out. Tybee took his time getting the camera together while their kids, Rachel and Luke began exploring the nooks and crannies of the strange desert terrain. They treated the barren landscape like a foreign planet, playing cops and robbers in outer space. Luke aimed his fingers at his sister. *Phew.*

Phew.

Nicole and her husband were too busy flirting with one another to notice the kids' disappearance into the orange haze. They searched the small curves and divots in the hills and eventually settled on splitting up to cover more space. Nicole was the only one who made it back to the van and found Tybee's smart watch shattered on the blacktop.

That seemed like ages ago. Another lifetime. Some heat-induced hallucination to distract her from the horrible reality she found herself trapped in. Now she was running for her life, running from the memories of her children's decapitated heads in the cave, running away from the sound her husband's howling screams, and running from the madman who was quickly gaining on her.

In college, she ran track and field where she received numerous comparisons to a gazelle with her long-toned legs and smooth stride, but that was more than a decade ago. In the interim, she had lost her graceful form and washboard abs. A good chunk of that muscle had turned into fat and she could feel it slowing her down. A profound sense of danger coursed through her nervous system and she wondered if she had been reduced to prey or a potential survivor.

When did I let myself go, she thought, cursing her laziness. *Running used to be your life. Now you're two steps away from getting slaughtered.* She could almost feel the ghost of her former self leaving her in the dust with a cloud of laughter.

A thin stream of sweat trailed down her spine and curled into the small of her back. She whipped the bulky camera off her neck, thinking about the happy memories stored inside, and tossed it onto the sand. Free of the weight, she was able to take longer strides, searching for some sort of cover and respite from the heat.

She threw a quick glance over her shoulder and saw the wiry man slowing down to inspect the camera, running his fingers along the extended lens.

Nicole took full advantage of the diversion and crouched behind a maze of sandstones. She twisted her sun-scorched body into a small space just wide enough to fit into. She pulled out her cellphone and jammed the numbers 9-1-1 into the dial pad to no avail. Her battery was in the red, teetering on the edge of death, and her phone was growing hot to the touch. She dialed the numbers again and again.

She slumped down and wrapped her arms around her bruised knees and fought back the tears. Leaning her head back against the rocky surface behind her, she stared into the blue sky.

Somewhere nearby, her discarded camera shattered against the sandstone. Nicole flinched. She took breaths as she heard the wiry man sniffing the air.

Lifting her left arm up, she smelled herself. A hint of lily perfume and body odor.

Jesus Christ, let me live. I'll pay my taxes on time, start donating to charities, and work on becoming kinder and more open. Please.

Shoes crunched in the sand with each step. They felt far away, but still too close for comfort. Nicole wanted to scream, wail out in frustration, but instead she bit her lip. She saw the man drop down on all fours, scanning the ground for movement. She clamped a hand over her mouth willing him and his black ponytail to look in the opposite direction. His head swiveled back and locked in on her.

She whimpered. Wedged in between two huge rocks, she managed to scoot backwards a couple feet. The wiry man slipped his long muscular arms through the opening and reached for her ankle, slipping out of his grasp. Grunting, he got down on his tattooed belly so he could stretch his arms in farther. He latched onto her other ankle and dragged her ass out as she clawed at the unyielding sand.

Nicole lashed out and kicked him in the kneecap. He cringed and released one of her legs. His grip on her other ankle remained firm and he brought his hand to her throat and squeezed. Her cheeks became ruby red and her head swam as she felt her life slowly leaking out of her body.

The wiry man squeezed harder, adding his full weight. Spittle sprayed from Nicole's thin lips as she honed in on his brown eyes before seeing a shape flicker inside his iris. She stopped struggling beneath his python grip and receded deeper into her mind. She thought of her kids and her husband, flashes of random people she interacted with over her short lifetime. Kids, friends, old lovers, homeless people, strangers all flared in her mind before slowing down and settling on a one-eyed dog—a Yorkshire Terrier limping in an alley. She saw it when she was five, wishing to take it inside and take care of it. She wondered if that same scraggly dog sensed her untimely death approaching back then. She had heard stories about a great white light at the edge of your demise, but all she felt was an unbearable heat sinking into her pores, burrowing into her bones, burning away everything in sight until all she saw was a singed darkness.

...

When the wiry man sensed her spirit leave her body, he wiped the sweat from his head and released a drawn-out sigh. She felt so much lighter now that she was dead.

She looked lovely and serene in her yellow sundress. He knew The Collective would enjoy her tender meat, but he held a deep appreciation for females—especially the dead ones. A familiar urge stirred in his lower extremities. Andrea would have disapproved of this, but she wasn't here to stop him, and he deserved a reward for all of his effort.

The wiry man stripped down. He smiled as the desert wind caressed his tanned skin. He gently pulled the bottom of the dress and rolled it up to her belly button. Tearing away the thin fabric of her panties, he dived into her rank pussy with his tongue. He savored the divine peach, slobber running down his chin. He couldn't have blamed Adam for eating that apple in the Garden of Eden. Shit, who wouldn't want to eat something so tempting and fresh.

He wiped the juice and pubic hair from his cracked lips. He opened her legs wider and played with himself before entering the folds of her vagina. It was a little dry so he pulled out, cupped an ample amount of her warm piss on her leg and stroked his shaft. Thoroughly lubricated, he slid back inside.

He opened her eyelids with his index fingers and stared into her cerulean eyes. He always held a genuine appreciation for classical facial structures and hers was a beauty. With each jagged thrust, he traced her sleek jawline and imagined her dissolving into the sand, melting away into a silky, brown oblivion.

He grew tired of missionary position and rolled her onto her side. He spread her ass cheeks and tried sliding inside, but she was too tight. Agitated, he smacked her right butt cheek leaving a red imprint of his hand. He fished his blade out of his jeans and sliced into her thigh muscle. Blood sluiced out, sparking in the sunlight. He cupped the blood and used it to lubricate his cock. He slid back inside and went to work as he curled her long black hair around his fist. He fell into a steady rhythm zeroing in on the sound of skin smacking skin and started a fresh mantra.

"Om Shreem Hreem Reeshua Namaha."

In between fervent thrusts, he repeated the words again with a great reverence, focusing on the vibration as well as the pussy. He grew painfully hard and an electrifying tremor ran up the base of his cock. He closed his eyes as he came and pale stars shuddered in the darkness behind his eyelids.

He pulled out and thanked the universe for his fresh kill.

"Namaste."

1.

Jesus's oversized plastic head bobbled wildly on Jerry Weiss's dashboard as he cruised down the empty desert road. He'd lived outside of Vegas for two years, yet he never visited the Valley of Fire. One of his co-workers called him lame for being such a homebody and not getting to know the lay of the land. That seed embedded itself under his skin and watered with time and contempt, grew into a tree of disdain. He wanted to be accepted and this slight had to be remedied.

Jerry paused outside the entrance to the state park, waiting for the park ranger to come out. A full five minutes passed before irritation set in and he had to confront the heat. He left the car running as he got out and inspected the area. Inside a small shack, a radio played old-school rock music and a fast-food cup was sweating in the heat.

"Hello? Anyone around?"

A fly smacked against the window repeatedly. looking for an exit.

"Guess not." He poked his head around the small structure, making sure he wasn't missing anything.

He contemplated driving off and taking the risk, but wondered about the possibility of cameras perched in covert locations or some other means of surveillance recording him. Maybe this was a test from up high to see which direction his moral compass would sway or a heady dose of paranoia. Either way, he fished out a soggy twenty-dollar bill and slid it underneath a sci-fi novel sitting on the desk.

Getting back into the driver's seat, Jerry shifted his weight, accelerated, and got back on the road. He stared in awe as the scenery slowly shifted from blurry shades of rust red and bold chalky white to a runny orange. The landscape was foreign to his city sensibilities, but it was so damn mesmerizing. He had never seen anything like it. Maybe it was good to get out of his box and explore nature for once.

Jerry hummed an old church hymn, muttering some of the words, losing himself in the strange scenery. "Jesus is mine...a foretaste of the divine." He nodded his head along to the melody and drummed his

GRANT WAMACK

fingers on the dashboard. Soon enough, his car putted to a stop. His humming trailed off and he looked at the gas gauge. The white needle pointed to "E."

He slammed his fists on the steering wheel and sighed deeply.

Everything's all right, he thought. *Just a minor oversight. I'm in God's hands now. There should be a gas station somewhere nearby. I'm sure of it.*

Jerry got out, popped open the trunk, and fished out an empty gas container. He set it down and slammed the trunk. Before he could forget, he opened the passenger door, grabbed his pocket bible, and slipped the well-thumbed book into his back pocket.

He walked down the road and, after a good ten minutes, took off his designer jacket and draped it over his right shoulder. Loosening his tie, he cursed the heat and knew he'd have to drop these off at the dry cleaners much earlier than anticipated.

Eventually, he came across a parking lot on the side of the road, a stop for tourists looking to snap some photos. It was crowded with all manner of empty vehicles, candy wrappers, food debris, and liquor bottles poking out of the sand like a flag. He anticipated seeing families awkwardly posing and children scrambling up rocks, but no one was in sight. Nothing but sand and rocks surrounded him for miles.

"Helloooooooooo?"

His shaky voice echoed off the rocks, disappearing into the endless expanse of desert like the waves of heat rising from the cars and trucks into the burning sky. After a few moments of walking around the parking lot, he suddenly felt utterly alone.

Maybe they blew up.

Jerry laughed at his grim humor. He had no idea why people drove miles to take crappy photos of colorful rocks. Can't believe he let his co-worker peer pressure him into this journey into the desert.

For what? Disappointment and heat?

Feeling down and out, he kicked a rock, trying to let his frustration out. He wished he was back home lounging in his air-conditioned apartment and tending to his houseplants.

Then an unlikely idea—small and burgeoning—blossomed in his mind. Something he would've never considered if anyone else was around. Something he would've otherwise ignored, but the *wrongness* of the idea only heightened the thrill, thrusting him into that "dangerous" territory.

Jerry jogged back to his car and grabbed a hose out of his trunk (from a failed home improvement project) and an empty gas canister.

He surveyed the vehicles, searching for a ripe candidate, thinking he could siphon gas out of a full tank.

Surely, God wants me to survive and not perish in the desert, he thought. *That's what He would have wanted, right?*

He remembered one humid night, walking back home from a fast-food joint he worked at. His thoughts revolved around his upcoming college semester and he wondered if he truly was ready for the transition. Some of his burnout friends cruised up beside him, blasting punk rock music, and invited him along for a joyride. They passed around a bottle of cheap tequila, taking huge chugs, while the car snaked down the road. It suddenly ran out of gas.

Brian, the driver, got the bright idea to suck gas out of another tank with a hose and gagged as the fumes hit his nostrils. Spitting out a mouthful of gas, he said the taste wasn't much better than the tequila they'd guzzled down. Thinking back on the moment, Jerry wasn't sure if he had the hardened stomach to get the job done. He had cut back on his drinking significantly and made the switch over to wine. However, sitting out in the desert and drying up like a raisin wasn't too appealing, either.

Rings of sweat formed underneath his armpits as he got a closer look at the vehicles surrounding him. A large mustard-yellow SUV caught his eye and he basked in the shade it provided. He unscrewed the gas cap with sweaty hands and looked around one more time to make sure the coast was clear.

Laughter rippled through the air.

Jerry dropped the gas canister and looked for an exit, an escape from the openness of the desert. His heart drummed in his chest manically. He was caught. Had to be. He could already feel the cool steel handcuffs biting into his wrists, and rough, callused hands shoving him into the backseat of a police car. The shiny glint of the police badge reflecting the sun off its surface. Orders barked out from a man in shades and a freshly pressed uniform. He wouldn't do well in prison, God knows.

A little girl with sand caked on her oval face and a dirty sunflower dress stepped out from behind a scraped bumper of a beater, wiping away those frightening images Jerry harbored inside his head. She grinned, revealing a set of yellow teeth that should've resided inside the mouth of a seasoned smoker, not someone who still believed in mermaids and unicorns.

"What are you doing, mister?" She adjusted a marigold stitched into the headband wrapped around her ponytail.

Jerry frowned, mentally running through a list of lies until it dawned on him, he was speaking to a little girl. He didn't have to answer to her so he shoved her question aside. "Where are your parents?"

The girl chewed on something fleshy. *Crunch. Crunch. Crunch.* Smacking her thin lips and moving the bulge around her cheeks like an acorn.

"They're dead."

Her chewing annoyed him, but the blunt force of her statement threw Jerry off guard. "Oh God, I-I'm sorry." He exhaled. "Do you think you can take me to whoever's looking after you? They're probably worried sick."

The girl nodded and took his hand in hers. Her small hands were abnormally rough for her age. A step below sandpaper. Probably a tomboy, he thought. Nothing wrong with that.

They started moving forward, leaving the familiar comfort of the parking lot, and Jerry's Italian dress shoes sunk into the sand with each step. He was too busy worrying about whether or not he kept the receipt for his shoes to notice the girl spitting out a pink glob of flesh. Even if the sound registered on a subconscious level, he would've figured it was hard candy.

He had no idea how far his thoughts drifted away from the cold reality occurring on the asphalt behind him.

The desert rat twitched in the dirt, covered in blood and saliva. Small white bones jutted out from its side. Mangled beyond repair and missing large chunks of meat. A tiny black eye dangled from its pink socket, watching a line of red ants march toward it. The rat shuddered before the world turned black and the fire ants began to devour its carcass.

...

The sun's rays shined brilliantly through an arched rock formation on the side of the road. Blinding light spilled out. The two lane road moved in a wavy black line, looping between miles of desert, disappearing into the hazy distance.

"God, it's hot. Why did we think this was a good idea?"

"Road trips are always fun. I wanted to show you there's more than Vegas in Nevada. Here's some water. Drink up. Don't want you getting dehydrated out here."

Will Beaumont wiped the sweat from his brow, dug in the backseat of their broke-down '07 Honda Civic, and tossed a lukewarm water bottle to his girlfriend, Anca Prunea. He had no idea how long it had been sitting back there, but he didn't care. He knew it would shut her up and buy him some time.

She nearly caught it one-handed, but it fumbled out of her hands and landed on the road. Cussing under her mouth, she retrieved the water bottle and moved a couple strands of black hair from her face and curled it behind her ear.

"Thanks, babe. How much longer?"

"Twenty minutes more or less. Hard to tell."

"Can I do anything to help? I feel kinda useless just standing here. Existing, you know?"

"No. Just keep standing there looking pretty or you can have a seat. Up to you."

Anca grimaced and leaned against the driver's side of the car, playing with her phone.

Probably taking another selfie, Will thought.

Will scratched his curly blond hair and fiddled underneath the hood, wishing he had shaved. His facial hair wasn't thick by any means, but combined with the heat and sweat, it became aggravating. He wanted to scratch his face so bad. Just say fuck it to the grease and oil stains covering his palms like a lost Pollock painting.

He shot a glance at his petite Romanian girlfriend. She was a knockout. He wasn't sure how he pulled her or what made her cling to him so fiercely. He eyed her snug white t-shirt with a three-eyed cat imprinted on the front and the words *Grizzly Bear* scrawled underneath. He didn't care much for indie rock, but that band in particular didn't make his ears bleed and the artwork was cool. Plus, his girlfriend was good to him...unlike this car. He had learned a few things about cars from his old man and bits and pieces from auto class, but he had no idea what was wrong.

His old man's words swam into his mind like a lost friend. "Women are like cars. You have to take care of them...keep the fluids topped off, gas tank at least halfway full, but don't treat them too nicely or else they'll take advantage of you. Sometimes you have to get a little rough with your vehicle."

Will snickered at the gem and wished he could still talk to his old man in the flesh. He felt a slight strain on his heart and he shoved the emotions back down into a box.

No smoke. No weird humming. No ticking. Fluids were reasonably filled. Matter of fact, everything seemed fine. The car should have been up and running, yet it wasn't. He didn't want Anca to know this or the other doubts churning inside his mind. Chalk it up to hubris, but for some reason he felt like it made him less of a man. He lacked that mythological elbow grease that was supposed to flow through his masculine veins. Still, he had to do something quick. He was growing nauseous and his temples ached. The heat was starting to get the best of him.

...

"We're rolling, Redd. Make love to the camera."

"Shut the fuck up, nigga. Why do you always have to say that gay shit?" Korey adjusted his gray XL sweatshirt that read "TOO TRILL" in giant red letters. He didn't want his gut slipping out from underneath it.

"I'm sorry, bro. I'm just doing my job."

"Well, do it minus the bullshit. You know we've been trying to make this happen for too long," he said, with a mouth full of gold.

"Okay, okay," Scotty tossed his free hand in the air and shook his head. "I'll stop playing around."

Staring behind a pair of cheap shades, Scotty Leibowitz took a few steps back on the huge piece of petrified wood he stood on, while precariously balancing the camera's weight on his shoulder. He ran his free hand through his short, ruffled black hair. He wore a brown V-neck that hid none of his chest hair, and a pair of cargo shorts. Jagged stripes of yellowish-white cut through the red rock that towered over Korey—or, as he was becoming known in the rap game, Big Redd.

"How's the angle?" Korey yelled.

"It's good." Scotty gave him a thumbs up. "Don't worry, brother. I got you."

Korey mean-mugged the camera, showing off his gold grill. He contorted his fingers into strange positions, flashing gang signs and rapping about his struggle, the grind, fucking and dodging bitches, a dash of the occult, and gripping wood-grain. He slipped in a few esoteric lines for good measure. He had a menacing frame: 6'4, 320 pounds and a mean demeanor that screamed stay the fuck from 'round me.

Scotty watched Korey take off his limited-edition Chicago Bulls snapback and fan himself with the hat. The rapper paced back and forth, sweat collecting in his short black dreads with the tips dyed a cherry red.

GOD'S LEFTOVERS

He warned Korey about the heat, but his friend was never one to listen. He was a rogue, a true individual if there ever was one and that's why he liked working with the man so much. In an industry full of fakes and wannabes, Korey was the real deal and inspired him to put together some intriguing visuals for the artist.

"Fam, I wish I could take off this sweater. I'm dying in this bitch."

"I told you to wear a t-shirt, but you kept on and on about wearing this sweatshirt."

"It's dope, though." Korey grinned and pulled out his phone. "Don't you think?"

"It's nice. Still, I'd rather not sweat to death. Life doesn't revolve around fashion."

"Tell that to Kanye, nigga."

"You might be right. Let's get back to it. My batteries won't last forever."

Scotty switched up the composition, watching Korey fill the frame. He adjusted his focus and aperture, and signaled a thumbs up. Korey moved his body through the desert as if he'd done this a million times over. Scotty recorded a few more minutes, editing the video in his head, chopping up the footage, and yelled "Cut!"

"Glad we're done. Feel like I'm about to melt out here. The next shoot is going to be somewhere nice and cool. Maybe someplace like Alaska. This place is for the birds."

"You did good. I'm excited about how it'll turn out. And give the Valley some credit. This place really makes you stand out." He scrolled through a number of frames on the LCD screen before shutting the camera off.

"I just need to get some aesthetic shots and I'll have everything I need."

"Bet. Just wish you'd get some water bottles too."

"I hear you loud and clear. I'll grab a couple water bottles from the car. All you have to do is chill."

Scotty walked a mile to get back to the car. He wiped the sweat off his forehead with the bottom of his shirt and could smell his own body odor wafting off him. He popped open the trunk and changed into a fresh t-shirt, cursing the all-natural deodorant he switched to at the recommendation of his hippie aunt. Relieving himself of the camera's weight, he could finally take a break and get some much-needed water in his system.

"Good ole' fashioned H2O," he said aloud. "Here's to you."

He toasted the air and something heavy slammed into the back of

21

his head. Black dots floated in his vision and the water bottle flew out of his hand, rolling underneath the car. Staggering forward, he turned around to face his assailant, but was knocked out by a swift left hook to the temple.

A shimmering halo radiated around the head of the figure approaching. He grabbed Scotty by the arms and dragged him into the desert.

2.

"What the fuck, Will? Thought you could fix this." Anca's Romanian accent was thick and heavy. It came out when she was angry and open with her emotions.

"Look. I'm frustrated too, but I'm trying my best. I don't know what you expect me to do?"

Anca frowned and crossed her arms. "Ugh, I never had these type of issues in Romania. Men know how to fix things there. Good with their hands. Maybe American men are a different stock."

"Bitch, you were dead broke in Romania. Sucking dicks and fucking any guy who would throw a euro your way. Don't tell me this is so much worse."

"You're an asshole." Anca spat at the ground.

"A wise man once said it takes one to know one."

"Fuck is that supposed to mean?"

Will waved his hands back and forth. "Know what? Fuck it. I'm outta here. You can fix the car yourself. Call one of your Romanian men and see if they can get a visa and come help. Weak stock my ass."

"You can't be serious, Will. You're just going to leave me? Alone. In the desert?"

"Watch me."

Will turned around and began walking down the road. He wasn't serious, but he had to stay faithful to his role. Sometimes, you have to be a hardass to keep the upper hand in a relationship. He knew Anca would follow. She couldn't stand the idea of being alone.

Will didn't even have to look back to confirm his theory. He could already visualize the tears welling up in the corner of Anca's eyes. He heard the signature sniffle and her hurried steps pursuing him and he grinned.

"I'm sorry, Will. Honestly, I'm sorry."

"How sorry?"

"I'm sorry much."

Will laughed, grabbed her face with his oily hands and kissed her deeply, sticking his tongue down her throat.

"Will!" She wiped away a portion of the black smudge from her cheeks and scrubbed her hands on her denim shorts. She searched for her pocketbook mirror, forgetting it was in the car. "How am I going to get this shit off my face? I look like a nihilistic clown. Like something in a Ligotti story."

Will shrugged. "I kinda like it. Adds a certain *something* to your pretty face."

"You're lucky I like you and your blond head." She embraced him, rubbing his lower back, and massaging the bulge in his pants.

He gripped her wrist and pulled her hand away from his zipper. "Not a good time, babe. I want to fuck around, but we need to figure out how to get back on the road."

She nodded. "Yeah...you're right. What now?"

"That's a good question."

A scream broke out in the distance. Will's member became limp and Anca's head whipped around like a pinwheel.

The scream rippled through the cigarette burnt sky and only intensified the second time around.

...

Korey replayed the video over and over in his head. The visuals would be quirky and unique while maintaining that core street element that kept his fans coming back for more. Simple supply and demand. The video was going to do numbers. He was sure of it. The top influencers, bloggers, and tastemakers would eat it up and he might possibly break free from the underground cesspool of rappers and move out of the city. The record deal had to be what came next.

What the hell is taking Scotty so long?

Growing impatient and hungry, Korey started back toward the car. He passed a number of limestones and large rocks riddled with caves. He had a feeling he was being watched from the wavering darkness even though he hadn't seen anyone besides Scotty's pale ass in hours. He considered checking the cave to be sure, but his gut told him to steer clear.

His uneasiness motivated him to pick up the pace and soon enough he was back in the small parking lot. He found the driver's door slightly open, but there was no sign of Scotty.

"Scotty! I'm not playing with you. Where the hell you at? Your mom obviously didn't raise you right. Leaving doors open and shit."

The wind howled.

"Stop being petty next door. I don't know why you always gotta play games and turn into Rey Mysterio. If you don't come out, you won't get the other $500 I owe you."

Korey waited for Jerry's cheese-eating grin to appear out of nowhere, but soon enough he realized he was all alone. Hating the silence, he took off his sweater and threw it in the backseat of the car which felt like an oven. He slid into the front seat and messed with the knobs on the radio, but forgot he didn't have the keys.

"Shit." He slammed the car door. "I just want to hear some music. Is that too much to ask for?"

He felt ten times more comfortable in his white wife-beater, but longed for the sound of thumping bass and treble. Music drove away the memories of frequent drive-bys, warbling police sirens, gentrification, and his aunt's constant nagging. More importantly, it softened the buried memories of friends, family, and lovers shot down on the east side of Chicago. The only thing besides music that offered any escape from his broken past was the sweet high Mary Jane provided.

He dug underneath the driver's seat, skirting past receipts, old fast-food bags, random trash and clasped around a plastic bag—the baggie of weed and rolling papers. The kids called this particular strain loud—slang of the moment for high quality weed. He carefully distributed the weed on the rolling papers, straightened the dried leaves into a horizontal line of green, and rolled. After sealing it with his tongue, he nodded, satisfied with his handiwork.

Fishing a lighter out of his back pocket, he lit the joint. He inhaled and blew out a thick plume of smoke. A few more tokes and he already felt better. The tension melted away from his body and his head felt lighter than before.

He glanced down at his shoes to assess how much damage the desert terrain had done. The gritty sand scuffed the hell out of his four-hundred-dollar kicks, the coveted Yeezy Boosts, but he stopped caring about the condition of his soles when he noticed the small drops of blood glistening on the asphalt.

He took a long draw from his joint, enjoying the small moment of static pleasure before dealing with the bullshit at hand. It had been a long day of filming, an even longer drive, but the sight of blood stretched it out to dizzying lengths.

What the hell happened? He smelled trouble and played with the idea of dipping out the Valley, but he didn't want to leave his friend alone in the desert. Scotty was aggravating at times, but he always came through when needed most and loyalty was becoming a rare quality these days.

Time to put in some work, he thought grimly and stubbed out the finished joint. Ashes embedded in the asphalt like a distorted sigil.

Korey grabbed the heater from the backseat, tucking the worn 9mm Ruger pistol into his waistband and headed off into the desert, following the trail of blood.

...

Jerry looked down at his cellphone to check the time, but it was acting wonky. The numbers kept shifting into a static mess and the signal was going in and out. Times like these he wished he owned a solar-powered watch instead of relying solely on his cellphone. Could have been a great investment. He looked up at the glaring sun, shielding his eyes, and wondered if he could figure out time the old way.

Who am I kidding, he thought? *As soon as I get this girl back to her parents, I'm leaving this horrible place.*

By now, Jerry couldn't see the parking lot or any other signs of life besides himself. The girl was a warm figure, tightly holding his hand. Sunspots hovered on the outside of his vision, painting a tangerine hue on the edge of everything. He rubbed his eyes and the sunspots multiplied.

"Are we getting close?"

"Yeah," she said. "Are you okay? Your eyes are turning red."

"I'm okay. Might be my allergies acting up."

"Okay mister... listen. You can hear *them*."

"Hear what?" The only thing he heard was the sand and rocks shifting beneath their feet and the occasional gust of wind.

"You're not listening," she said, in a sing-song tone and the slightest bit of sarcasm.

Jerry strained his ears and just when he thought this was another childish game—he heard *it*. A long, drawn-out chant combined with a subtle moaning that slowly transitioned into actual words. They seemed foreign, maybe even ancient. Slow harmonic strings of syllables. Deep vibrations took root inside the soles of his feet and rapidly travelled up the ridges of his spine, settling into the base of his forehead.

The sound only intensified in volume and pitch as they approached the source. Jerry became aware of how sweaty his hands were and wondered if the girl noticed his nervousness. His bald head tingled in the worst way as it too broke out in a sweat. A slow burn erupted across the top of his head as the skin started to peel back from the slow onset of sunburn and became inflamed.

"Isn't it beautiful?" she asked.

He gently patted his head with his free hand, hoping he could extinguish the stinging heat. "W-what?"

"The music, silly. I know you hear it."

"Yeah...it's just strange." He wanted to drop this girl off as quickly as possible and be done with the deed. He wasn't sure what to think about this music. It made him feel heavy and thick, lethargic even. It was most certainly the devil's work the way the notes filled the empty spaces in his head, and his heart pulsed.

"Don't worry, mister." She squeezed his hand. "They don't bite."

"I hope not. Do you know these songs?"

"I know a few. I'm still learning. I think they're called..." She sounded the word out. "...man...man-tras. They're fun."

Jerry smiled weakly and turned his attention to the group of people they were approaching. It seemed like a small camp of people sitting in a loose circle cropped by a set of huge rocks. There were about 12 or 13 people, he estimated, sitting in cross-legged positions with their eyes shut, meditating, in the middle of the desert. Behind them were a set of dome-like tents arranged in offset rows. Weird symbols were painted on the tents that made the hairs on the back on his neck stand at attention.

He bit his lip, concerned about the child's well-being and wondered if child protective services would even travel somewhere this far. *Might be best to take seat and observe before taking sudden action*, he thought. *I'm on the Lord's time. No need to rush.*

"Are those your caretakers?"

The little girl nodded and he muttered a small prayer for the child.

One woman seated in the center of the group with a multi-colored headdress stood up. She looked to be an authority figure of some type in the way she carried herself with a strange sort of regal energy, taking long strides as she approached Jerry. Sandy-brown hair with streaks of blonde running through it hung down her back and she wore a light brown t-shirt and oversized round black sunglasses that hid her eyes. She seemed a little on the thin side, but she was fit.

She spoke with an accent he couldn't quite place. "What brings you here?"

"This might come off a little weird, but I found your girl playing a game of hide-and-go-seek in the parking lot. Seems like she lost her way. Thought it would be a good idea to help her get back to camp. I assume she belongs to you?"

The woman stared at Jerry for a moment, licked her chapped lips, and cracked a smile. "Yeah, she belongs to us. Not sure how she got out of eyesight, but it happens. In any case, I appreciate you bringing her back. That says a lot about your character."

Jerry extended his hand and she shook it firmly, with a surprising amount of strength. Her hands and wrists were covered in exuberant turquoise bracelets and rings. Shaking off the pain, Jerry felt awkward, not really sure how to end the conversation and felt antsy to get back to the relative safety of his car.

He scratched the back of his head. "I haven't even introduced myself...I'm Jerry."

"Nice to meet you. I'm Andrea, and that lovely group of people goes by the name of The Collective." She gestured to the circle of crazies who looked malnourished in one form or another.

"What exactly are you guys doing in the desert? Camping or something?"

"We're on a meditation retreat. Astrologically, it's the perfect time to get in tune with our inner selves."

"Oh, I see...but why? I thought people usually went camping in the woods?"

"We've done meditation retreats in the woods too. It's good to switch up the locations. Move outside of your comfort zone. Allows you to really grow and discover parts of yourself you've been estranged from."

"Right."

"You know what this place is?" She gestured to the sand and the tents.

"Yeah. The Valley of Fire."

"You're correct." She snapped her fingers. "But do you know the significance of the land you're standing on?" She stomped on the ground for dramatic effect.

Jerry shook his head, readying himself for the lecture he felt coming like a storm. Still, he was a bit curious.

"The Valley of Fire is a sacred site. Old land dating back to prehistoric times. Lots of dormant energy here. Spirits, entities, old souls. Compared to the soullessness of the concrete city, it's prime real estate to meditate and connect with something *real*."

"How long do you plan on staying here?"

"As long as it takes."

Jerry frowned and cracked his sweaty knuckles.

Andrea caught on. "Listen, I'm sure you're thinking I'm speaking nothing but new age mumbo jumbo and I understand. We're just meditating. Think of it as therapy. Only difference it's free. It would be great if you joined us for a bit."

"I'm not sure." He glanced back towards the horizon. The company he worked for held a few meditation classes, but Jerry always declined. He didn't think it was right and worried it went against his religion in some subtle way.

"You certainly don't have to, but I really think you should. We have some good people with us, and I can get you some water. You look flustered."

Jerry started to give into her sincerity. He could use some water and his car wasn't going anywhere anytime soon without gas.

"Follow me," she said.

...

"Help me!" Scotty screamed.

A few minutes earlier he had woken up in total darkness. Battered and broken, his entire body ached. He felt a sharp sting in the myriad of cuts that originated in his ass and branched down his legs. Blood trickled from his wounds and he bit down on his bottom lip, grains of sand burning like salt.

"Someone help me. Somebody. Please..." His voice echoed off the cavern's walls and eventually faded away into the darkness. His vocal cords felt strained and scratchy. A bundle of useless dry twigs taking up space in his throat.

No one came running as he had hoped. No one responded to his cries of distress.

He never had much of a voice in school. Whenever confronted about his quiet tone, he blamed it on what he referred to as quiet kid syndrome, the typical introvert. His camera became a vessel for his voice, his vehicle for expression. His directorial skills brought him the attention he craved and satisfaction from his peers. Just a few hours ago, he thought this video might bring him and Korey the success they both doggedly pursued. He never imagined himself shooting music videos for independent artists, but he was sure all routes led to the same goal: Hollywood.

Palm trees, fast cars, glistening watches, a nice villa, stacks of cash, little-known islands, business suits, and pretty women dominated his vision board back at home. It sat above his ratty mattress and gave him the drive to get out of bed every morning. He had no idea how his grand vision had led him into a world of pain and flashing lights. That wasn't part of the plan. Far from it.

With a grunt, Scotty grabbed onto a large rock for leverage and lifted himself off the ground. He leaned his heavy head against a rough wall, relishing the coolness it provided. He stepped forward and nearly collapsed. His legs were more fucked up than he thought.

"Take it slow," he muttered. "One step at a time."

Darkness surrounded him and he only saw the dim outline of his surroundings. Something dripped down from up high. *Must be in a cave*, he reasoned.

How the fuck did I get here, though?

There were some psilocybin mushrooms in the car, stuffed in a baggie hidden in the glovebox, but he didn't eat them yet. His dealer said they were high quality and would bring on some trippy visions. He was saving them for a celebration he was beginning to doubt he would get to experience. It was supposed to be the psychedelic cherry on top of the shoot.

A memory flashed through his frazzled nerves.

Incredibly strong arms dragging him through the desert. A wiry man with a featureless face silhouetted by the sun. Small jagged rocks tearing into soft flesh. Blood spilling into the sand like red rubies. Swallowed up by the quiet sand dunes like a snack.

A pervasive rage boiled inside Scotty's gut and scorched his mind. He wanted to *hurt* that man. Shell out pain on scales unheard of. He hadn't been taken advantage of like that since his freshman year in college. That motherfucker was going to pay.

The only question was how and how long did he have to wait for the man's return?

And where was Korey?

God knew he could use the man's help.

3.

"Fuckin' bullshit," Korey muttered.

The trail of blood had disappeared. People don't just up and disappear. Especially those who are hurt and bleeding. Scotty had to be around here somewhere. He surveyed the area, searching the nearest sandstones for any sign of human life, but there was absolutely nothing.

It was almost too clean. Made Korey feel like something was off and his intuition didn't lie. It guided him when he was at his most high and his most low points of life. Couldn't turn his back on his gut now. He had to follow it, let it steer him in the right direction.

Korey walked in circles, orbiting some imaginary anchor point, until he grew dizzy. He sat down on a flat rock, needing to get his head right, and lit a cigarette. He cursed himself for not grabbing the rest of that weed earlier. His high dissipated rather quickly after finding Scotty's blood. He inhaled deeply, contemplating the next move. Search some more? Call it a day and go home? And what exactly was he going to do when he found Scotty and his kidnapper (if there was a kidnapper)?

This could be a major troll on Scotty's part. Some sort of prank. He fucked around with him on numerous occasions and vice versa. They fought like brothers and shared a weird kinship. Still, this didn't fit Scotty's frame of humor. He wouldn't try to pull off something so grandiose, and neither one of them garnered enough fame to be on a prank show in the middle of the desert.

Korey took another pull of the cigarette, slowly accepting the situation and realizing what he might have to do. It'd been a few years since he killed a man. He could still see those watery brown eyes staring at him accusingly. The body bucking in the alley as it gave up the ghost. Blood pooling in a pothole. He tossed the cigarette, kicked some sand over it, and watched the cherry disappear with the ghosts of his past...for now.

He sat listening to the wind blow sand across the desert floor, but it carried something else with it—a slight humming that made the hairs on his neck stand.

Korey stood and followed the sound best he could until he spotted a group of people huddled together in a rough circle. They sat on top of blankets and pillows, tents behind them. A woman wearing an elaborate headdress was speaking to man in a business suit while a little girl was playing in the sand. Who the hell wears a business suit in this kind of heat? Still, he was relieved there was actually someone else out here, living and breathing like himself. Maybe they could help him find Scotty.

Korey traced his finger along the pistol in his waistband. It had belonged to his older brother before he was shot down by a trigger-happy gangster disciple anxious to prove himself and gain some clout. He could almost feel his brother's corporeal presence taking a weight off his broad shoulders, reassuring him from the otherside.

The voice of Korey's dead brother rumbled through his head. *"Don't trust anyone of these niggas. Doesn't matter how nice they dress or how sweet they smile or how well they speak. Give them a reason, an opening, a moment of vulnerability, and trust will get you killed."*

He nodded and took a deep breath, knowing he wasn't alone in this. Not one to rush into a situation, he crouched down and hid behind an arched rock. He pulled out a fresh cigarette, thought better of it and slid it back into the pack. *Save that for later,* he thought, *might be needing a helluva smoke break when it's all said and done.* He sat down in the sand and leaned back, waiting for the sun to drop below the horizon.

...

Scotty had been walking for what seemed like hours in near darkness, cutting his feet and collapsing a number of times. He spotted a smidgen of light and he hurried along awkwardly, forcing himself to pick up the pace despite the sharp pain in his legs.

He moved along the wall, feeling the grime smudge across his palms and the heat intensify ten-fold as soon as the sun touched his face. He took in a breath of fresh air, happy to be nearly free of the damp cave.

A silhouetted figure blocked his path and Scotty groaned, realizing this had to be the same man who dragged him inside the cave. He sobbed as he staggered backward, falling on his ass. In the face of his enemy, all of his anger had melted away and he was weaponless.

The wiry man strode into the cave wielding a heavy-duty flashlight. Sharp knives dangled from his waist and clanked against one another. The steel gleamed in the sunlight. He moved in quick and delivered a nasty left hook, re-opening the cut on the side of Scotty's face. Warm blood trickled down his cheek.

Scotty countered with a weak jab, barely grazing the man's abdominals. Unfazed, the man simply grinned and brought the flashlight down Scotty's shoulder blades. That did the trick. He picked Scotty up as if he were a small child and threw him over his shoulder. Scotty struggled, digging his nails into the man's upper back and then resorted to biting his neck, sinking teeth into ruddy flesh. The man yelled and dropped him.

Scotty landed on his side and nearly lost consciousness, but the wiry man's heel forced him back into the present. He spat out a glob of blood as well as a tooth.

The wiry man delivered a swift kick to Scotty's ribs over and over until he heard a satisfying crack. Scotty cringed, holding his side, readying himself for another blow. However, the sound of his own blood rushing through his throbbing head and the sheer force of the beating pushed Scotty into a darkness much deeper than that of the caves. It reminded him of the womb—warm, wet, and comforting.

Scotty came to, staring bug-eyed at the ground with the stark realization that he was hanging upside down. He tried to move, mumbling positive affirmations to himself, but felt something snug around his ankles, securing him to the ceiling of the cave. Gravity clawed at his consciousness, attempting to drag him down farther into the darkness.

The wiry man sauntered over with a short blade in hand and a tin bucket in the other. He set the bucket down beneath Scotty's head and unclasped a serrated knife from his waist. He gently ran it along Scotty's exposed chest, the steel softly touching his skin with a fierce intimacy.

Scotty lost control of his bladder and warm piss ran down his waist, traveling down his hairy chest and over his gasping mouth. A few rogue drops were swallowed by the sand.

"Oh did the little man have to take a whiz?" the wiry man said. "The fun hasn't even started yet. Make sure you don't go shitting yourself. You'll ruin the flavor."

Flavor? What the fuck?

Scotty's thoughts cut off the exact moment the man submerged the knife into his stomach and were replaced by a hot nebula of pain. He watched as the knife was pulled back out and sliced downward, opening his upper body. Blood spilled out in rivulets, quickly filling the tin bucket and eventually seeping into his eyes. It felt like a thick shampoo, stinging his eye sockets and making it hard to breathe.

He spat out a glob of blood and was transported back to anatomy class in college. He remembered the brown spotted bullfrog he'd cut into seven years ago. The delicate veins, the glassy eyes, the slick mouth ready to reveal death's secrets. Secrets ready to cross that thin film separating the living from the otherside.

Scotty felt his insides sliding outward, gravity begging to release his organs. He thought back to his childhood when his father—a stern man with a sure hand—gutted a fish, efficiently slicing it open vertically, and disposed of the useless guts, tossing them back into the sea.

The wiry man crouched down, his lips scarcely brushing Scotty's ear, and his harsh breath caressed his cheek like a distant lover. "Don't worry. Your sacrifice won't go unnoticed."

The wiry man hummed as he continued making precise, almost surgical cuts, opening Scotty and handling him like a steaming walk-in closet: organs serving as upscale men's wear ready for consumption.

Scotty felt his equilibrium swing somewhere to the left as his life force spilled out and his spark extinguished. He ceased struggling and his body became still as he swayed from the ceiling. A butchered pendulum.

The wiry man licked the blood from his fingertips, enjoying the juicy, copper taste. There wasn't anything like it. Thanks to hard-earned experience, he learned that everyone had a slightly different flavor. Depending on skin health and diet, people held a fascinating array of textures.

The wiry man might as well be the cannibal equivalent of a wine snob—only difference was he dealt in blood. Lots of it. The thick liquid used to make him vomit back in his teens. He was so naïve and experimental in his youth. Took time for his stomach to build up its defenses and get accustomed to the taste. Nowadays, he could guzzle the liquid down like orange juice.

"Mmm, good stuff," he said, patting Scotty's carcass. "You'll make a fine meal. The Collective will be pleased."

...

Will had no idea why he was following Anca into the desert. He was certainly no hero. His dad tried to force him into the military. *Be a man like your dad and your dad's dad. Put on a uniform, grab a gun, and go into the field.* He couldn't do it. It went against his morals and deep down he knew he was a coward. When he graduated high school, he grabbed his shit and dipped out of town. He took his savings (a large sum handed down from his parents) and traveled to Europe where he thought he could find himself. Instead, he found Anca and everytime he looked at her it was a stark reminder of his past. He could feel his ancestors watching his every move, appraising his worth.

This desert felt like a heat-box and the sand was clutching every step, pulling him deeper into the earth. He wasn't built for this.

The only good outcome would be diving into Anca's sweet pussy later on in some cheap roach-infested motel room off the side of the road. He could bury himself in the folds between her legs and try to forget his dad's overwhelming shadow. Even now, he watched Anca's tight ass sway from side to side, appreciating the simple sight. Maybe he should have taken her offer earlier and let the girl suck him off.

He had been dating her for a solid year and things were enjoyable, but there were other *prospects* roaming the coffee shops he frequented. Young vibrant creatures ready to be taken out for a spin. It was hard to keep his interest fixated on Anca and not indulge his urges.

"Who do you think was screaming?" she asked. "You think someone got attacked by a coyote or something?"

"Maybe it was a coyote or some bozo gone off peyote and booze. Maybe some weird bird or experimental aircraft. I hear the military conducts a bunch of tests in places like this."

"Doubt it. We're in a state park. I don't think the government can do that here. They would get in trouble."

"You got me there. I have no idea. I'm just glad it wasn't us doing the screaming."

"Will, it shook me up a bit. And I get the feeling that someone needs our help."

Our help? He held back a nervous snicker. *You must have me confused with someone else.*

"Do you hear that?" Anca said.

"Hear what?"

"A weird humming. Kinda like cicadas but *different.*"

As if on cue, the humming drifted into his ear canals. "More like an obnoxious radiator."

"Probably has something to do with the screaming."

"Well, we're about to find out."

They passed a number of oddly shaped rocks, some with gaping caves filled with darkness. Will spotted a group of eccentrically dressed people sitting in a circle, meditating peacefully.

"There's your fucking cicadas."

Anca gave him the cold shoulder and continued toward the group. She noticed two people talking with a girl in tow and nudged Will. She headed in their direction, wanting some answers.

"Excuse me," she said. A bald man decked out in fancy business attire looked toward her. Another woman tilted her head, appraising Anca. "Hi, my name's Anca, and this is my boyfriend, Will. This might sound strange, but we heard a scream from the road. Is someone hurt? We're worried."

Andrea's smile fell. "No, I didn't hear any screams. We wouldn't be able to meditate with a disturbance like that. I don't think it should be dismissed though. I'll ask one of the members to look into the matter." She motioned toward the meditation circle.

The businessman looked like he could seriously use some sun lotion. The blistering heat had cracked open his dry scalp and his cheeks were red and ruddy. He seemed fidgety and it made Will paranoid. He wanted this guy to get the fuck away from him. Move out of his immediate circle and stay back.

"What's your problem?" Will said, gesturing toward Jerry.

Jerry stammered. "N-Nothing. Just hot, that's all."

Anca pinched Will's forearm. "Be nice."

"Is there anything else we can help you with?" Andrea said.

"Well, our car broke down. You know where we can find a gas station or do you think we could possibly get a ride?" Will hoped one of these hippies owned a vehicle.

"No, we biked our way here. If you want, you can borrow one of them to get back into town."

"That's a long ride. You seriously biked all the way out here?"

"No kidding. We did. Don't get me wrong, it was a long ride and we took a bunch of pit stops, but it was worth it. The Collective may not look like much, but we're strong as a unit."

"The Collective, huh? That's impressive. I don't think we could make that ride even if we knew where we were going."

"The offer still stands. I wouldn't want you two passing out from dehydration, though."

Anca gasped, and Will sensed the hopelessness wrapping around her.

"Don't worry. You can spend the night with us. We have food, water, and extra sleeping bags."

Will put his arm around Anca, and she leaned into him. He looked at Andrea again. She seemed nice enough. Pretty too. Might as well take her up on her offer. They didn't have any other real options.

"Sure. Why not? We'll treat it like a sleepover." Will feigned laughter.

"Yeah, that sounds like a good idea, but we don't want to intrude or anything," Anca said. "And we're low on money."

"No, it's no trouble at all. We love having guests. It mixes up the energy and keeps things from becoming stale. And I'm flattered you're staying the night. You two look like a spicy couple."

"We can be..." Anca laughed.

Will figured they might as well take advantage of a free meal and a goodnight's rest. "We'll stay the night, but we're heading out first thing in the morning. Don't like the idea of staying in the desert for too long. It's dangerous and hot as hell."

"Perfectly understandable." Andrea smiled warmly. "And how about you? You're welcome to stay, too." She turned her attention to Jerry, waiting for an answer.

"Funny thing is my car ran out of gas so it looks like I'll be staying the night, too. We're all in the same boat. How 'bout that." Jerry wiped sweat off the back of his neck with his hand nervously.

The little girl who everyone had forgotten jumped up and down, clapping her hands.

"It'll be a feast," Andrea said. "Can't wait to introduce you guys to The Collective. They'll love your vibes."

4.

The wiry man had been a butcher like his father and his father before him. It was something embedded in his DNA. Something that separated him from his peers. Something that drove him to pierce flesh, cut ligaments, and discard of bone and gristle.

He wiped his bloody hands on Scotty's discarded shirt and used it to wipe up away the dry skin on his lips. The cave's cool temperature would keep the meat relatively fresh for tonight's feast. He grinned at the neatly trimmed slices. Glistening ribs, fillets, and loosely cut meat and gristle laid on a small table in organized stacks.

Fishing out a syringe from his pocket, he tapped the sharp needle a couple of times before injecting a clear liquid into the meat. The drug was a wicked mix of chemicals meant to induce sleepiness and lust. It would then increase the levels of testosterone in the victim, creating an all-consuming need to fuck like animals on cloud nine.

He looked forward to the morning's festivities and smiled as he reminisced about the number of successful kills he pulled off. This ritual might actually help him surpass his grandfather in total number of kills. It was a dream of his to outdo his ancestry and make his mark. Something about catching something—whether it be an animal or a human—satisfied his primal urges. It made him feel more in tune with his Native American roots despite being only half Cherokee.

He carefully stepped over a pile of organized bones and headed back to The Collective. The sky looked as if someone took a cigarette and put it out across a purple background leaving behind vibrant orange streaks. Night was approaching.

...

Andrea walked into the center of the circle and breathed in deep, breasts rising and falling, whispering what sounded like a set of foreign words to the uneducated ear.

"What the hell are they saying?" Jerry whispered.

"It's Sanskrit," said Anca. "Old language."

Will furrowed his eyebrows. "Where'd you learn that?"

She shrugged as if it was common knowledge. "I'm not fluent, but I learned bits and pieces from an Indian man I dated back in Romania."

Will snorted. "There's Indians in Romania? Like Native Americans, or Indians with the red dot on their forehead?"

She punched Will's shoulder. "Don't be an idiot. You'll get us cancelled on social media talking like that. Anyway, Romania's beautiful and expansive. A lot of different cultures and ethnicities come there for work. And he wasn't Native American, he was an Indian from India. You dumb-dumb."

Members of The Collective slowly stood and stretched their weary limbs as if they just woke from a long overdue nap. A couple of them noticed the outsiders' presence and started whispering.

Andrea raised her voice so everyone could hear. "We'll be having guests for dinner tonight. Looks like they'll be staying with us for a bit. Treat them as if they're one of our own."

A lean man wearing a black bandana tied around his head came over and shook hands with Will, Jerry, and then did a slight bow for Anca. The others stood up, bones cracking, and introduced themselves.

The meditators were genuinely pleasant and overall comforting, despite being in the desert. They introduced themselves, some shook hands while others went in for a tight hug. For most of The Collective, the concept of a personal bubble didn't seem to exist.

"Now that we're properly introduced, it's time to eat." Andrea clapped her hands and motioned the guests to come over and have a seat.

The sky looked like it was covered in purple bruises and orange shades. Will and Anca held hands as they picked out cushions to sit on. Will settled on two red cushions with gold trimming and brushed the sand off his before sitting down and staring at the last rays of sunlight. He was glad that he would finally be able to cool down, but disliked how the long shadows stretched across the sand dunes.

Anca scooted over to his side and nuzzled her head into the crook of his neck, looking for comfort in the middle of nowhere. He brought his arm around her shoulders, bringing her in closer.

Will was curious as to what type of food they would be eating for dinner. He had a light breakfast with Anca and they shared some sandwiches they made the day prior for lunch. The sandwiches were a bit soggy, but failed to tide him over. He pictured the tuna seeping out the bread and almost gagged remembering an article about self-cannibalism that stuck with him throughout the years.

On a dental visit, he'd flipped through a random magazine and read about a group of hippo researchers who went missing and starved to death in the harsh jungles of Brazil. When the human body fails to find proper sustenance, it starts consuming dead cells from the tongue and cheek; then it moves onto the fat reserves and finally the organs. He licked the inside of his cheeks, tongue brushing the bottom of his canines, shaken at the possibility of the process already taking place. He didn't want to end up like those researchers literally eating themselves to death.

A couple of men helped a pregnant woman build a small bonfire with wood salvaged from the Valley. They added old receipts, torn socks and whatever else deemed unnecessary and lit the contents. The receipts sparked. A breeze nearly blew the spark out, but the flame took root and shot up into the air like an orange phoenix, fluid and wavy. Soon enough, the fire was crackling and started devouring the rest of the contents.

The sun had disappeared beneath the horizon and night swept through the desert, bringing with it a cool breeze and a bit of a bite.

A couple of women shared colorful shawls, cuddling together, taking in warmth from the fire.

"You look cold. Would you like a shawl? We have a few extra ones."

Anca nodded. "I would love one. Thank you. I didn't realize the temperature would drop so low. Wish I brought a jacket or something.

The woman wrapped the shawl around her shoulders, thankful for the added heat and the strangers' generosity.

A wiry man, covered in geometric tattoos, carried two huge plates of meat that looked like chicken and dry chunks of turkey. There were hints of gray in his long black ponytail, and crow's feet hung from the corners of his eyes. Perhaps he was in his mid 30s, but the crow's feet hinted at many years of hard living. Despite all this, a soft smile spread across his face.

"What kind of meat is that?" Jerry asked, salivating.

"Meat we gathered from the land. It's good, I assure you," Andrea said as she passed around paper plates and water bottles.

"Must be some gluten-free, organic types," Will snickered. "At least they eat meat."

"Sure doesn't look that way," Jerry said.

The fire emphasized how dangerously thin some of the figures were as they passed around plates of food. They looked as if they hadn't eaten in days and more than a few resembled ghosts wearing paper-thin sacks of skin. It was a wonder they survived this long.

Jerry glanced over at the little girl who seemed healthy enough. When she noticed him watching, she waved and dug into a bone thick with meat. She chewed with her mouth open, gristle and fat stuck in her teeth. It made Jerry's stomach turn.

He stared down at his own plastic plate that held a few chunks of meat. He picked at a small piece and nibbled. Similar to chicken's consistency and flavor, it tasted surprisingly sweet despite being somewhat dry.

"What is this?" Jerry said as he bit into an even bigger piece. "It's pretty good, but different."

Andrea finished chewing her food, before speaking. "Glad you're enjoying it. It's a combination of mammals we hunted and killed ourselves. Connects us back to our roots. Our ancestors."

Jerry nodded and inspected his meat once again. It looked fine. Still, he wanted a straight answer.

Will cleared his throat. "So why exactly is the...the...Collective meditating here of all places?"

"I discussed this with Jerry earlier. This ground we're sitting on," she gently patted the sand, "it's a sacred site. Natural and *mostly* untouched. Takes us back to an older time. It's much easier to get in tune with the gods and nature."

"Cool, but what do you mean by getting in tune?" Will side-eyed the group as a whole. They were pleasant and generous, but he liked shaking things up. It was a bad habit, but he loved it.

"Depends on what kind of route you want to take. We primarily focus on tapping into certain vibrations via mediation."

"Okay." Will furrowed his brow. He still had no idea what she really meant but was glad to have some food in his stomach. "Why are you called The Collective, though? You have special merchandise or something?"

The fire crackled and black ashes rose into the night sky, vanishing. "No, not at all. We're a band of gypsies, wanderers and nomads. In a lot of ways we're similar to the Aghori Sadhus in India. Many of us felt like outcasts at one time or another. We came together and found solace in one another."

"You're like a new age gang, just more peaceful," Will said.

Andrea shifted her weight and laughed. "We shy away from the term 'new age'. We're a little more complex than that."

"I think it's lovely that you started this community. Everyone deserves a home of some sort," Anca said, envying their familial bond. "I miss Romania."

"Yes, I'm glad you agree. And I hear Romania is gorgeous in the winter. I plan to travel there one day...I'm sorry, but I must excuse myself. It's getting late and I'm heading to bed. I advise you do the same. Big things are happening in the morning." Andrea stretched her arms and yawned.

The other members of The Collective mimicked their leader's tired movements and muttered amongst themselves.

"What's going on in the morning?" Jerry said.

Andrea stared at Jerry with her bug eye sunglasses until he started rubbing his head nervously. "The second half of the feast."

"I thought this was the feast?" Will spoke before Jerry got a chance to continue his barrage of questions. "Are we having a big breakfast or something?"

"Every day's a celebration. We have to cherish life while we still have it. Food is one of the best ways to really get to know one another. Connect. You'll understand tomorrow."

Andrea stood and helped collect the rest of the plates and water bottles, tossing them into a black garbage bag. "Grab whatever extra blankets and sleeping bags are available. I recommend you get a lot of rest. Don't stare at the stars for too long."

Andrea disappeared into the darkness of her tent and the three outsiders were left by themselves. The fire was beginning to die down. The chill increased and all three of them shivered, wondering what tomorrow might bring.

"We're hitting the sack," Will said to Jerry as he drew his arm around Anca's shoulder. "Don't stress. We'll be leaving first thing in the morning. You can come with us if you want. We'll find a way home."

Jerry nodded, envying them as they headed toward the sleeping bags. He sat alone, watching the fire shift and waver, becoming lost in the vibrant colors. He looked down at his hands that were snow white and trembling from gripping his bible too tight. He was unsure as to why he was shaking, but he had a feeling something bad was going to happen. Something about what the woman had said rang true.

5.

Will struggled to squeeze into the blue sleeping bag, despite it being made for two people. Anca was skinny, but he had to slightly rip the seam on the left side to fit his whole body in. He wondered if anyone would notice the tear in the morning, but he didn't care that much since it didn't belong to him. Once he managed to get inside, he felt tightly cocooned in cotton and polyester.

"This was a bad idea." Will sighed as he wrapped his arms around Anca's slim frame. "I'm telling you, they're a bunch of looney tunes."

"They seem like nice people. Stop being so judgmental." She stroked his hair, twirling his curls around her finger, and kissed him softly. "This is nice. Different from the norm. We just have to make it through the night and tomorrow we'll be back on the road."

"I hope you're right."

"I know something that'll make you feel better." She grinned mischievously as she unbuttoned his blue jeans and snaked her hand into his boxers, wrapping her fingers around his hard cock.

"You know me too well." He leaned back, enjoying the way she cupped his balls with one hand while working the shaft with the other. She smiled and her mind drifted back to her days as a sex worker—seemed like a lifetime ago.

She met him at a grimy whorehouse in Amsterdam. She thought he was cute and sidled up to him after he had ordered his drink. She flashed her smile, a smile that would make men pull out their wallet without a second's notice. He grabbed her hand and asked how much. Hook, line, and sinker. She knew she had him. However, he came back day after day, slowly getting to know the ins and outs of her life. She spilled her story to him, the ups and downs, not sure what it was about this backpacker that triggered this release. One day, she got up, grabbed her things (which wasn't much at all) and left with him. She never looked back.

Anca had a working visa now and worked as a secretary for a

company that refurbished old gaming systems. It was boring, but better than sitting around the house. And anything was better than having sex with random strangers for money.

The wiry man with the ponytail walked by and paused, looking lost. Anca watched him lock eyes with her own and she shivered.

"Do you need something?" Will asked.

"Yeah, I'm hungry...and horny."

"Well, it looks like you're out of luck."

"Oh, I highly doubt that." The wiry man pulled out a short blade.

Anca gasped and nearly ripped Will's dick off. He grabbed Anca's hands and squeezed them hard.

They struggled to get out of the sleeping bag. The seams continued ripping. She thought she might be able to defend herself if she could get on her feet. She'd fought plenty of men in Romania and learned how to hold her own in conflict.

The blade hovered above Will's throat and came to rest on his Adam's apple. His dick went limp and he ceased to struggle.

"Don't either of you scream or that'll be the end."

"Hold on, hold on." Will breathed heavily. "Aren't you supposed to be peaceful? I-I don't understand why you're doing this."

"I am peaceful, but a man has needs. You're a man, you should empathize with me." The wiry man glanced at Anca's lean body and licked his lips.

"Listen, I can give you some money if you want. I even got some euros on me. J-just let me get my wallet out."

"No, I don't want your filthy money. Your dead presidents won't bring any of us closer to God. What else can you offer?"

Anca watched Will rack his brain for ideas. She knew what the crazy motherfucker wanted, but didn't want to accept it. She couldn't.

"How about I let Anca suck you off since you're horny? I can't do anything to bring you closer to God, though. That's out of my hands."

Anca glared at Will. "What the fuck, you asshole? I'm not sucking anyone off. What do you think I am?"

Will gulped, Adam's apple brushing against the blade held to his neck. "Just suck his dick, Anca. He's about to slit my fuckin' throat."

"What do you say?" The wiry man rubbed the bulge in his pants, eye-raping Anca.

Anca couldn't believe Will. She thought he loved her. She gagged, already imagining how horrible this man's dick would taste in her mouth. She'd sincerely believed her dick-sucking days were long behind her, but she was right back in the thick of it. The man who held the knife up to Will's throat was obviously out of his mind. He would most likely kill her (soon to be ex) boyfriend and have his way with her afterwards.

She sighed. "I'll do it, but no swallowing."

"You got yourself a deal." He snatched Anca's hand and dragged her out of the sleeping bag.

"You don't have to be so rough." She dusted herself off.

"Tell that to your boyfriend." He pulled her into the darkness.

She looked at Will for some sort of help or consolation, but he looked away, acting as if she didn't exist. She felt like he had changed or maybe she was starting to he him for who he truly was.

"Fucking bastard."

The wiry man undid his pants and pulled out an enormous cock. The stench hit her in waves of putridity. It smelled like a combination of spoiled milk and bad meat. She gagged and held her hand up to her mouth.

"It'll be okay," he said. "You're a strong woman. I'm sure you've experienced much worse than this."

He was right; she had experienced worse, much worse, but that didn't make the situation any better. That was the past, the same past she worked so hard to distance herself from. A couple continents and a body of water's worth of distance. Now she was thrown right back into that hellish reality. She dropped down to her knees, wishing she had her old switchblade on her. She'd cut his dick off in a heartbeat and laugh as he bled out on the desert floor.

Anca wrapped her hands around his dick, took a deep breath, and stuck his member into her mouth. He moaned, grabbed her head for leverage, and shoved it in even deeper. She struggled to breathe as he fucked her throat ragged.

Tears ran down her cheeks and a long strand of pre-cum spilled out of her mouth. He pulled out and she breathed heavily, gasping for air.

"Ready for more?"

She moaned in abject terror and he took that as a yes. He shoved his cock right back in between her luscious lips. He closed his eyes and failed to notice her left hand blindly comb the sand behind her and fingers wrap around a jagged rock. She hid it behind her as he pulled back and caressed her hair. He kissed her and she slammed the rock into his cheek the moment he pulled away. It connected with his nose and something crunched. He fell backward, clutching his ruined face.

"You bitch!"

Anca leapt on top of him, thinking about every single man who used her for money, and brought the sharp rock down on the wiry man's face repeatedly, until it caved in and blood gushed out of the crater formally known as a face. The excessive amount of blood splatter brought her back to the present and she let go of the rock with a trembling hand. She breathed heavily as she attempted to collect herself.

She felt exhausted, arms heavy, and crawled back toward Will's blue sleeping bag. The bastard was gone. He ditched her, hoping he could make a run for it.

Sand shifted in the distance, and Anca watched dark shapes undulate beneath the dunes like giant serpents, but were soon buried by a strong gust of wind. She closed her eyes and let darkness take over.

...

Andrea watched Jerry from the shadows. She could tell he was a weak shell of a man and his fear was so palpable it made her wet. She slid her hand into her cotton panties and moaned as she rubbed her clit in a circular motion. After reaching the point of an orgasm, she ventured out of the shadows and revealed herself.

"Didn't peg you as a night owl," she said.

"Ugh, not really. Just catching up on some reading." Jerry gestured towards the Bible in his hand.

"Oh, that's good to hear. It's a shame not too many people read much of anything these days."

Jerry nodded, not really sure what to say. He was still concerned about tomorrow and how he was going to get home. Maybe he could borrow one of those bikes and ride out to a gas station. He could use the exercise.

They both stared at the fire and she looked at Jerry and grinned. Her sunglasses reflected the dying embers and he felt his heart rate speed up and his breathing grow heavy.

"I thought you were tired." He hoped he wasn't being rude.

"I was, but sometimes I like to walk around at night. Clears my mind."

"I understand. Similar to what I'm doing."

"Yeah, I figured I could get to know you better."

"Oh yeah?" He stared at her lopsided grin.

"Come walk with me. I want to show you something. I have a

feeling you'll like it."

"Where?"

"Just come on. Where's your sense of adventure? It'll be a surprise. Don't be scared, you'll be with me. I'll be your guide."

Shoving the Bible in his back pocket, he stood up and followed her lead. She grabbed his hand and pulled him away from the fire into the darkness.

"I can barely see anything. Do you know where you're going?"

"Yes, don't worry so much. Loosen up. You have to learn how to trust others. I've walked around these stones plenty of times. This valley might as well be my home now."

"How long have you been here? I mean you and The Collective."

"Long enough."

He swallowed hard and wrapped his hand around the wooden cross hanging from his neck and asked for strength. He almost tripped as he was yanked forward and just barely managed to regain his footing before falling into the darkness surrounding him.

"Seriously, where are we going?"

"Nonstop questions. We're going to look at some art."

"In the desert?"

Andrea paused for a moment and sighed. She dragged him along in silence. Jerry almost tripped a number of times, nearly bringing Andrea down with him.

Eventually, they stopped in clearing surrounded by a huge pile of rocks and sandstone crags.

"Here we are. Atatl Rock."

"I don't see any art...is this a trick?"

"No, we just have to climb some stairs and then we'll be surrounded by the art. It's awesome. You have to see it."

"I didn't know I was going for a hike today, or else I would've brought my running shoes."

She laughed. "You wore a fancy jacket and dress shoes to the desert. What kind of sense does that make?"

"It's my first time, okay. Give me a break."

"Just this once. Come on, before it gets any colder."

Uttering those words seeming to trigger something in Jerry. He shivered and wished he had grabbed a shawl or two to keep him warm. The temperature change was drastic, bordering on frigid conditions. He wasn't sure how Andrea was wearing shorts and not freezing her ass off.

They made their way up the stairs, gripping a steel hand-railing which was cold to the touch. Jerry felt the steps warp and wobble underneath his weight. He started hyper-ventilating.

"These stairs are too flimsy." He wanted to turn back, but the distance seemed way too far.

"You're seeing things. Just take a deep breath and hold on to me if you need to."

"Okay." He wrapped his arm around her shoulder.

"We're almost there," she said.

Jerry looked at the dark mounds on the horizon. He knew they were gigantic sandstones, but something about their presence made him uneasy. He saw the raw outline of a deformed elephant with a trunk that sloped down in a way that defied physics and an alligator with knobby scales running along its sharp spine.

"Jerry, are you still here?" Andrea asked, bringing him back to the stairs, back to the present, back to reality.

"Yeah," he croaked.

"We're here."

"I still don't see any art."

"Let me." She grabbed his hand and guided his fingers over the rough indentations in the wall up to the diverse petroglyphs imprinted into the rocks. His fingers moved in spirals, and then he felt the outline of lizards and turtles. "Sublime, isn't it?"

"Yeah." He was in awe of the petroglyphs. Back in the city, he went to a couple of art exhibits, but was never able to get this close to the art and actually feel it with his own hands. He felt like a kid again.

"These are about 3,000 years old. Native Americans stood here." She stomped her feet for special effect. "And carved these figures into the walls. I wonder if they knew the petroglyphs would survive to this day and we would be here to appreciate their efforts."

"It's incredible."

She still held his hand and pulled him towards her. She kissed him and moved her hands behind his back.

Jerry pushed her away. "Stop. We shouldn't be doing this."

"Why not? Are you a taken man?"

"No, but I'm in service to God."

"I'm sure God wouldn't mind if I borrow you."

She grabbed his tie and ripped it off his neck, letting the wind snatch it away. It flew into the darkness. She pushed him against the wall of the rock, kissing him roughly, biting his bottom lip.

Jerry enjoyed the softness of her lips and the warmth emanating from her body, but the situation was dizzying. He felt like a fly engulfed in a spider's delicate web and he was coming to like the experience more than he should.

He shoved Andrea off him and ran down the stairs, ready to return to camp. *I'm being tested right now*, he thought, growing short of breath. *My morals have to stay intact. I have to get back to camp.*

He looked back to see if she was pursuing him and he tripped over his own legs, rolling down the last flight of stairs. Feeling like one big ball of hurt, he massaged his knees and his neck. Even with the pain taking over his senses, he managed to hear Andrea slowly make her way down the steps.

Clank. Clank. Clank.

"That didn't work out, did it? We were having a good moment, a nice connection, but you wanted to ruin it. It's okay, I forgive you."

She climbed on top of him and he struggled to throw her off despite being twice her size.

Andrea dug her fingernails into his shoulders as she pushed him down into the sand and kissed his neck, giving it a slight bite with her upper teeth.

"What the fuck?" He gingerly touched his neck and saw blood on his index finger.

"You don't like a little pain?"

"N-no, I don't. Why—"

She backhanded him and laughed as she took off her shirt, revealing small tits that hardened in the cool night breeze. Even though Jerry wanted nothing to do with this woman who reeked of musty earth and incense, his cock grew hard in his pants. Andrea rubbed her cheek against the bulge and absorbed the warmth surging through his pants.

"Oh, you like this. Stop pretending. It's good to indulge your shadow side every now and then. Makes you more whole and authentic."

She ripped open his white button-up shirt. Buttons flew in the air and rolled into the darkness beyond the base of the stairs. She rubbed her soft tits on his chest as he scooted backward, looking for some sort of respite from her overwhelming sexual energy.

While laughing, she gripped his collar on both sides and pulled him back towards her. Pinning him to the ground with her knees, she reached over and grabbed the Bible.

"Hey, that's enough," he said, reaching for his prized possession.

She dusted the sand off the cover, licked her thumb, and flipped through the pages. "You really believe this stuff, huh? What about the

Quran, the Bhagavad Gita, the Tripitaka? Are those irrelevant?"

Jerry couldn't even speak. He stretched his arm out, straining for the book again.

"I guess this has all the answers? The key to life, right?"

Jerry felt helpless underneath her weight. All he wanted was the Bible, but he knew the book would do nothing to protect him from this woman.

"You don't like me reading your little stories? Little allegories Mommy told you when you were a young naïve boy. Shit, who am I kidding? You're still naïve. I bet you're a hotshot businessman. A good Christian man. An upstanding citizen. I'm sure your clients or your boss get wet every time you quote scripture. Am I right? No answer. That's fine. I have another question for you. You ever just look up at the sky and stare at the stars?" She gestured upward, cupping her chin with her free hand. "And dream of that mythical place called heaven? I mean, we all do at one time or another."

"Yes," he whispered, wishing he was in God's kingdom. Heaven's gates awaited him. He was sure of it.

"What's that? I couldn't hear you over the wind. Sounds like you're conflicted. Having some doubts."

"Why are you doing this?"

"Oh, being a good host? Taking you in, giving you shelter? Showing you art? Feeding you? Is that what you mean? Letting you experience my body?"

"I mean..."

"You mean what?"

Jerry stared off into the dark sky, hoping someone would save him, but he knew he was alone and the woman's words were searing pinpoints, seeping into his skull.

She bent down inches from his face, her nose nearly touching his. Her sunglasses reflected his horrified expression. Bags under eyes. Chapped lips. Sallow skin with a thin layer of sweat.

"You know we have much more in common than you think?"

He shook his head, not accepting what his eyes were taking in. Her hair was moving on its own volition. The strands resembled a cluster of snakes hissing and moving their curves towards him.

"I used to be religious. Used to go to an all-girls Catholic school. Oh yes. Used to get down on my knees like a dirty slut and pray to that big man in the sky. But did he ever respond? No. When my dad broke my sister's jaw, did he listen then? Was some form of karmic punishment dealt out? No. So I turned to other gods, other deities. Different avenues of reaching the divine. I just wanted proof that there was more than this." She opened her arms, gesturing to the Valley. "All I really wanted was a glimpse beyond the veil, but I think I failed...thankfully there are other ways to reach God. He sleeps inside all of us, waiting to be embraced."

Andrea ran her fingers down his chest, tarantula-like, until she reached his belt buckle and undid the clasp. She unzipped his pants and licked the rim of his belly button.

Jerry lay there, mesmerized by her hands. They seemed to multiply, leaving phantom images trailing behind her movements. He wondered if he was sick or if the food he ate gave him food poisoning, but this was unlike anything he had ever experienced.

She smiled when she whipped his cock out, nearly devouring it. Her head bobbed up and down as she tried to take it whole, feeling it tickle the back of her throat. She gagged and came up for breath.

The snakes in her hair were in a frenzy now. Their thirst still wasn't quite quenched.

"I figure we might as well have a little fun before the end comes. Am I right?"

Andrea pulled her shorts off and tossed them aside, and did the same with her organic panties. Her unshaven pussy was moist, ready to be filled. She fingered herself, savoring the moment. Then she slipped his cock inside her and moaned as the man grew harder. The moan washed over him like a wave that lasted far too long.

She straddled him, forcing him to thrust deeper as she furiously rubbed her clit between her index and middle fingers. She sped up, enjoying the thrill, losing herself in the moment. Suddenly, she orgasmed and fell on top of him dramatically, resting her head on his chest.

Listening to the machine-gun beat of his heart, she moved to his ear and licked it before biting a chunk of cartilage off and swallowing it whole.

Jerry cried and his hand went to the left side of his head, attempting to stop the blood from leaking. His head felt extra heavy, and he wasn't sure if his neck and shoulders could support it. He shoved Andrea with his free hand but she didn't move an inch. He clenched his fingers into a fist and struck blindly. It connected with her face and she reeled back.

Dumbstruck by Jerry's punch, Andrea gingerly touched her nose and it came away red. She grew angry, struggling to regain that mindfulness she worked so hard to achieve during her strict meditation regiment. She inhaled and exhaled through her lips rapidly and released a deep sigh.

"Almost lost control," she said. "I still love you nonetheless."

Jerry stared at the calm face that hovered above him, not sure if this was some sort of ruse or something else entirely. She was out of her mind. He knew that much. Her expression failed to waver, and a couple drops of blood dripped down and landed on his exposed chest, running down his stomach, finally coming to rest inside his navel.

That's when he noticed the blood caked around his pelvis. It smelled terrible. He noticed the blood consisted of swirling patterns: sacred geometry and Fibonacci sequences. It was fascinating until he realized where it came from.

She registered his sickness and grinned. "It's exactly what you think. Divine residue from the Mother. Ancient legend says this blood can open portals to other worlds, other dimensions. Perhaps we won't be the only ones feeding tonight."

Jerry's eyes widened and rattled around his sockets as he moved backward. The patterns became more defined and pulsated. Andrea yanked his cock, showing him who was boss. She was going to find God by any means, even if that meant devouring him piece by piece.

A large shadow enveloped her, and Jerry watched it flicker red and black over and over. Sand particles floated in the air. Goosebumps rose on his arms.

Jerry watched Andrea spin around, facing a lithe naked woman, whose facial features were hidden behind a white cloth with zigzagging red stripes draped over her head. She sat atop a pale muscular horse. It snorted, digging its hooves into the sand.

Standing up, Andrea made a dramatic show of dropping to her knees and bowed to the ground before her goddess. Tears streamed down her cheeks as she was overcome with joy at finally achieving her dream of bringing a deity into this dimension. She shoved her pinky into her mouth and licked the blood from her fingers one by one.

The naked goddess spoke, but not in anything resembling human language. Instead, she emitted a high frequency hum that shot into Andrea's cerebral cortex and fried her brain cells like ants underneath a magnifying glass.

Andrea screamed and crumpled to the ground, clutching her head as the sky quivered and the stars threatened to rain down.

...

Korey woke up to a scream. His neck hurt and his whole body ached from falling asleep on uneven rocks. He rubbed his hands over his face and tried shaking himself awake; slowly recalling the day's events.

"The fuck?" Korey muttered when he noticed the sun slowly rising and the sky filled with shades of bruised purple and dirty yellow.

He stood up wearily, cursing himself for sleeping through the night and made his way in the general direction of the meditation group he spied earlier. They had to know what happened to Scotty. He hoped his friend was still alive and that they could return home but a small voice inside him said differently. Despite the doubts, he promised himself a fresh blunt, a bottle of Henny, and a Swedish massage if they made it back home with his friend in tow.

The remains of a fire crunched underneath his feet and Korey gasped as he came across a dead man wearing a fancy suit. A pool of blood surrounded his head like a crimson halo and the air smelled like shit. What truly stole his breath was the old man with liver spots who straddled the businessman's dead body. He pulled out a never-ending stream of intestines, wrapping them around his neck like gold chains.

Not one for magic or sick cannibalistic fucks, Korey pulled out his pistol and shot the man through the back of the head. The old fuck slumped forward and fell into the sand. The shot's echo was deafening, and he was sure others were well-aware of his presence. He didn't have much time and doubts dug at the edge of his thoughts as he moved forward, mentally preparing himself for whatever else he was bound to stumble across.

Head throbbing from dehydration, Korey moved through the sweltering heat and checked how many bullets he had left as he saw limbs twisted together in a sick display of sex and feeding. He had to put an end to this madness.

An anorexic woman with a shawl wrapped around her shoulders rode a half-naked man who sported long brown hair and a goatee. She scooped out handfuls of bloody soup from his torn stomach, hungrily devouring the bits of meat floating inside. She turned around and moaned as she grinded her pussy against the man's limp dick.

"Am I glowing with His presence yet?"

"No, bitch."

He let off a shot into her face at point blank range. Her nose disintegrated as a hollow-tip bullet ripped through her nasal cavity, briefly lodging itself into her ethmoid bone before exploding into a sunburst of shrapnel, completely wrecking the inside of her head.

Mentally checking off the kill, Korey glanced down at the two bodies before him, waving off the flies that were already beginning to gather. Slightly sick, he closed her eyelids with trembling fingers out of respect to the dead, half-expecting her to leap back up despite the leaking hole in her face.

Waves of distorted flesh moaned as they rose out of the sand, threatening to devour him. He thought he was hallucinating when he noticed the sheer number of body parts that littered the ground like ancient artifacts. A spattering of brightly painted toes, a shoulder blade, a glistening ribcage, and other ligaments lay in the sand. Might as well have been a slaughterhouse.

Adrenaline flowed through his veins as he shot into the orgy, bullets ripping through sweaty flesh, brain matter, and cushions. Then he recognized the blond guy from earlier. He was too busy gouging out another man's eyes with a thin stick to notice Korey. But where the hell was his girlfriend?

Something clawed at his ankles and Korey kicked back instinctively and jumped out of harm's way. It was the pretty European girl, except her legs were missing from her thighs down. She was covered in bruises and small cuts as she managed to drag herself forward using nothing but her arms and willpower. Her eyes were wild, darting back and forth, reminding him of dustheads he'd seen wildin' out in alleyways back home.

It looked painful the way she moved, exposed bone and entrails sliding through sand like a cluster of wet tails. Whatever she was on must've been strong enough to mask the pain she was experiencing. Korey had to put her out of her misery. It was only right.

He fired off a shot that landed inside her upper chest and her head snapped back. She fell to the sand face-first and blood flowed freely like hot lava.

Korey turned his sights to the blond guy, who crouched over the blind man beneath him. The blond guy took his hard cock, stroking it before he shoved it inside the man's orbital cavity, eye-fucking his way past the cornea and busting through the lens. Bits of tissue and nerve cells splattered on his pelvis as he pulled out. Screams rang out across the valley.

"Sick fuck," Korey muttered as he cocked his pistol and let off a shot. He missed. Taking a breath, he steadied his aim and took another. It ripped through the blond guy's head and sent him straight to oblivion. The blind man wrapped his large hands around the dead man's cock and ripped it off with a grunt. Blood geysered from the wound and rained down him.

Sobbing slick with blood, the blind man pushed the dead man's body off him and bit into the bloody cock like an ice cream cone. He struggled to stand, but managed to find his footing and stumbled awkwardly through the darkness, searching for the man who fired the gunshots.

Korey watched in awe as the blind man groped through the air, but he managed to shake off his brief reverie and squeezed the trigger one more time, blowing the man's brains out.

Where the hell is Scotty? He has to be around here somewhere, or at least his remains. Something. The man deserves better than this.

Korey checked each of the tents, killing any other murderous goofies he came across. Part of him wasn't sure if it was a dream, but the ringing in his ears and the smell of cordite brought him back to reality every single time.

A strange figure slowly emerged from the heat like a mirage straight from hell. Korey rubbed his eyes, thinking he was hallucinating, but the figure continued forward and his unstable features shuddered into focus.

The wiry man's bruised face was caved inward. His nose was twisted into a bloody S and pointed toward his right eye, chock-full of burst capillaries and emphasized by a black ring.

The man reminded him of a weird kid who lived down the block when he was younger. His neighbors liked to make fun of the poor kid, calling him terrible names like retard and squash face. The kid's face was misshapen from a terrible accident. Car accident maybe. To makes things worse his cousin even joked around, calling the kid God's leftovers. Some type of genetic failure that somehow made it out the womb in one piece.

The only problem was this person in front of him was far from a helpless kid on the block; this was a full-grown man who had survived the worst and was coming his way.

The wiry man carried the remains of a female leg in his hand, gripping it right above the bruised flesh of the ankle. Large chunks of muscle were missing, most likely being digested in his rigid stomach.

Korey raised his pistol, pulled the trigger, and heard a distinctive *click* that reverberated through the silence. His heart skipped a beat and sweat beaded on his forehead.

"Oh shit. This can't be happening."

"Out of bullets, huh?" The wiry man grinned, taking a few practice swings with the leg. He could certainly do some damage based off the way he swung from the hips.

Korey fingered the trigger over and over despite being out of bullets. He thought the gun might be jammed, but he knew that wasn't the case. He had simply miscounted his shots.

He smacked the gun, willing it to function properly. "Work, motherfucker, work. I need you to work just this one time."

"I used to play baseball. Little League. That was obviously a long time ago, but I think I still got it. Muscle memory, I think they call it. Let's test this theory out."

The wiry man charged and swung the leg at Korey's head. He missed. Wind brushed the top of Korey's head as he ducked down and his red-tipped dreads flew upwards in slow-motion. He rose and pistol-whipped the wiry man across the jaw. The wiry man flailed into the sand. The bloody leg slipped out his hand and landed somewhere in the distance. Korey kicked him in the chest one good time, but the second time the wiry man wrapped his arms around his ankle and pulled him down like a massive oak tree.

The gun slipped from Korey's hand and skidded into the darkness of an indigo bush.

Despite being mutilated and half-blind, the wiry man moved quickly, and delivered a jab to Korey's kidney. Korey took a sharp breath through clenched teeth. The wiry man pulled Korey's wife beater upwards exposing his gut and a mound of fat. Blood streamed down his chin and he smiled with a sick satisfaction.

"Awww." The wiry man licked his lips. "I can tell you have a lot of gods writhing inside you, *fat boy*, and I intend to release every single one of them."

Korey screamed and smashed his forearm into the wiry man's face, temporarily stunning him. He climbed on top, pushing his weight on the man's bird-like chest and grinned when he heard him struggling to breathe.

The wiry man threw his hands out, wildly scratching at the air. He connected with Korey's face, ripping away skin from his cheek. Korey roared out in rage, rage at the desolation he faced his entire life, rage at his brother's untimely death, rage at the loss of his friend Scotty, rage at the scorched desert, and most of all, a hot searing rage directed at the wiry man beneath him who dared to take his life. He brought his fists down in a blind fury, pummeling the man's face inward until he heard bones crack and his hands were completely covered in blood.

A weird silence settled over him.

Sweating profusely, he looked down at what he had done and thought he would vomit, but instead he felt a strange sense of relief wash over him. No one else was coming to take his life—or anyone else's, for that matter. It was done.

Korey walked through the desert with a limp, searching for the parking lot or a sign of Scotty's missing body, but found neither. The man deserved a proper burial.

Dehydrated and woozy, he stumbled through a number of heat waves that seemed impenetrable, pushing him back from the parking lot. He fought through, step by step, until he passed out.

He woke up, coughing up mouthfuls of sand and grit. He felt like he'd been baking in the sun for days and imagined sand coursing through his veins, drying him from the inside out. When he looked up, he found a naked woman riding a pale horse, looming over him.

"Join me," she said without moving her lips or opening her mouth.

The words felt like warm eels moving through his head. He pinched himself to make sure this wasn't a dream or a weird side effect from being out in the desert too long. He stood up and she offered him a hand. She was surprisingly strong and helped him climb atop the horse's back, which was covered in thick red and white blankets. Each blanket had special patterns sewn into the design. Irregular shapes enclosed in circles that made Korey's head hurt. Thick arrows and spears stuck out of the horse's backside like the spines of a cactus.

In silence, they rode farther into the desert. Korey wrapped his arms around the mysterious woman's waist, wondering what her face looked like underneath the thin cloth. He was sure she was beautiful.

"Do you know where we're going?" she asked.

"I-I have no idea."

"We're going home."

They crossed stretches of sandscapes and there came a rumbling deep within the earth. A rhythmic vibration that almost threw Korey off the back of the horse. He managed to hold on, while the goddess seemed unperturbed by the tremors.

His gold fronts began to vibrate, and his mouth rattled so hard he forgot how many stacks he had wasted on them. His gums bled and he tasted copper.

Rocks rained down a large mountain in the distance and he almost forgot about the pain in his mouth. The goddess calmly guided the horse around the boulders. A monolithic dragon composed of large sandstones rose from the earth and sand rushed down its sides like a dirty waterfall. It slowly stood on its haunches.

A sound akin to large chunks of chalk being broken in half filled Korey's ears as the dragon opened its dry ragged mouth, revealing a large fire raging inside. Shadows danced inside the light.

The naked goddess directed the horse to walk straight into the flames, and Korey clutched her waist even tighter as they entered the dragon's mouth. His skin crackled and popped, and his flesh slowly slid off his charred skeleton like a worn suit, but he felt at ease holding onto the goddess.

Thoughts of home welled up in his mind as they left this world and disappeared into the next in a fiery blaze.

ABOUT THE AUTHOR

Grant Wamack is the author of *A Lightbulb's Lament*, *Black Gypsies*, and *Notes from the Guts of a Hippo*. He has had more than 40 short stories published in places such as *Dark Moon Digest*, *The Best of Surreal Grotesque*, and *The New Flesh*. When he's not writing, he's reading Tarot cards, managing music artists, and smoking weed in LA. You can visit his website here: http://www.grantwamack.wordpress.com.